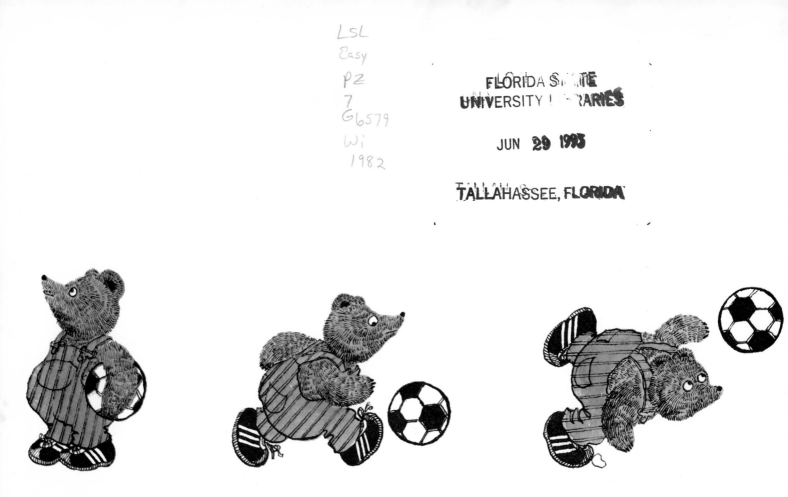

Library of Congress Cataloging in Publication Data

Gordon, Margaret, 1939-   Wilberforce goes on a picnic.
    Summary: Brief text and illustrations depict activities from sunrise to sunset the day Wilberforce and his family go on a picnic.
[1. Picnicking—Fiction.   2. Bears—Fiction] I. Title.
PZ7.G6579Wi   [E]   82-3476
ISBN 0-688-01481-X   AACR2

Wilberforce

GOES ON A PICNIC

MARGARET GORDON

William Morrow and Company
New York 1982

One day Wilberforce went on a picnic.

He woke up Grandmother and Grandfather,

and he had an enormous breakfast.

Then he cleaned his teeth and brushed his ears.

Grandmother packed the picnic.

Grandfather started the car.

Waving good-bye to Mother and Baby,

off they went through the town...

and then through the country...

until they found an ideal picnic spot.

Wilberforce found a puddle,

and then a pond,

and then Grandfather found Wilberforce.

Grandmother unpacked the picnic,

and they all ate until they were full.

It got rather windy,

and then it began to rain.

Grandmother cleared up the picnic.

Grandfather started the car.

Off they went through the country...

and then through the town...

until they reached home.

Wilberforce had a hot drink and a bath.

After supper he went to bed.

Grandmother and Grandfather finished supper,

and then they went to bed too.